> A MODERN RETELLING OF *LITTLE WOMEN* <

MEG, JO, BETH, *AND* AMY

A Graphic Novel

L B

Little, Brown and Company

New York   Boston

To Louisa May Alcott,
a writer I love.

And to my abuelita, Catalina,
who taught me what family means.

—Rey

To my brothers and sisters,
who motivate me to be the best
versions of myself. To my
parents, grandparents, and
friends' parents, who all believed
in my dream. And to my wife,
Tamiris, who has stuck with me
through thick and thin.

—Bre

CHAPTER 1

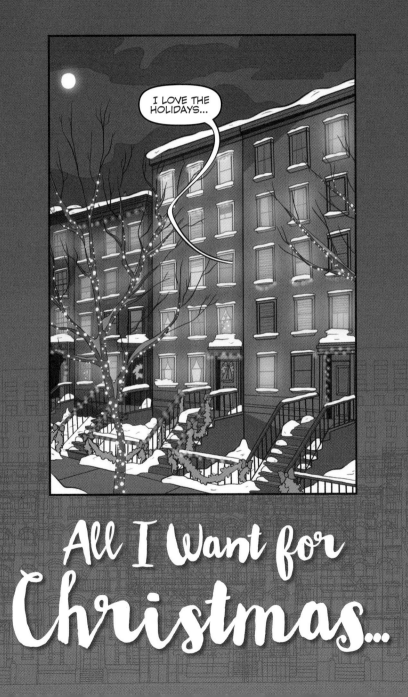

All I Want for Christmas...

DO YOU THINK IF I CLEANED THE HOUSE EXTRA GOOD MOM WOULD GET ME A GUITAR?

HAH   HEH   HEH

THAT'S AS LIKELY AS TARA CONNOR *NOT* MAKING FUN OF ME AT SCHOOL.

WHAT ARE YOU TWO COMPLAINING ABOUT? AT LEAST YOU DON'T HAVE TO *WORK* ON TOP OF GOING TO SCHOOL. TUTORING *AND* BABYSITTING IS THE WORST.

I'LL TRADE YOU. ANYTHING IS BETTER THAN WORKING FOR AUNT CATH. SHE'S A CRAZY PERSON— AND COLD AS ICE.

I HAVE AN IDEA! INSTEAD OF BUYING GIFTS FOR EACH OTHER, WE SHOULD ALL BUY PRESENTS FOR *OURSELVES.* THAT WAY WE GET EXACTLY WHAT WE WANT.

I THINK THAT'S A GREAT IDEA...

FROM: Robert March
TO: Madison March
SENT: December 19

How are all of my girls? Thanks for sending pictures of family pizza night. I can't believe how much all of you have grown in only a few months. The pics made me very happy…and very homesick. I know it's been hard, having me away, serving in the army, but it's the honorable thing to do, not just for you, but for our country.

People in America think they have it hard, but they are far better off than many. I have seen so much suffering over here. Some have lost their

homes, some have lost their loved ones, and some have lost everything. War is nobody's friend. But I believe in what I'm here for: making the world a safer place for each of you.

I hope all of you are behaving and taking care of each other. Make sure you take care of your mom too. Be good, my little women. I love you with all my heart.

–Dad

I KNOW,
SWEETIE.
IT'S JUST
HARD.

I HAVE AN
EARLY DAY
TOMORROW.
I'M GOING
TO BED.

GOOD
NIGHT,
GIRLS.

CLICK

CHAPTER 2

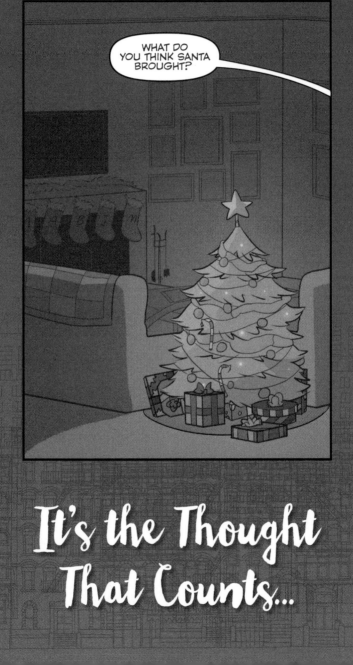

It's the Thought That Counts...

FROM: Megan March
TO: Robert March
SENT: December 28

Hi Dad,

Christmas wasn't the same without you. How could it be? This is the first time I've had the holidays without you.

Remember our first Christmas alone together? When it was just the two of us in that little apartment in the Village after my mom passed away? I insisted Santa wasn't real. You kept telling me he was, trying so hard to give me a good holiday. So much that you rented that ridiculous Santa outfit and that big white beard. I guess you knew me well enough to know I'd stay up late to catch a glimpse of Jolly Old Saint Nick. But your well-laid plan backfired!

You were all, "Ho ho ho, hello, little girl, I'm Santa!" I think you expected me to jump with joy. Instead, I screamed! You were shocked, but come on! I really thought you were an intruder in our apartment. I don't think you realized how terrifying it would be for me to find a stranger in our living room. I screamed so loud, I woke the neighbors and they came to make sure no one was being murdered. Ha! You must have been mortified.

I can't tell you how relieved I was when you pulled off that beard and hat. I cried until my tears turned into laughter. Then we had cookies and watched the snow fall outside. It's still one of my favorite memories. I'll cherish it forever.

I miss you so much. I know what you're doing is important, but I selfishly wish you were here with me.

Send

At least for the holidays.

Love you, Dad.
XOXO, Meg

P.S. Attaching a picture of your "little women" in
front of the Rockefeller Center Christmas tree.

CHAPTER 3

How NOT to Ring in a New Year...

OKAY, A FEW RULES BEFORE WE GET TO THE UPPER WEST SIDE...

...IF YOU START SAYING SOMETHING DUMB, I'LL SCRATCH MY LIP. IF YOU'RE BEING RUDE, I'LL RAISE MY EYEBROWS. IF YOU START TALKING ABOUT POLITICS, I'LL—

YOU CAN MAKE WHATEVER FACES YOU WANT, BUT I'M NOT GOING TO PRETEND TO BE SOMEONE I'M NOT.

JO, PLEASE DON'T EMBARRASS ME. THIS PARTY IS FULL OF THE COOLEST PEOPLE I KNOW. AND SOME OF THEM ARE RICH. WHAT IF I MEET MY FUTURE HUSBAND TONIGHT?

WHAT IF YOU MAKE ME BARF SAYING DUMB STUFF LIKE THAT?

YOU'RE ONLY 17. WHY WOULD YOU EVEN BE THINKING ABOUT MARRIAGE?

IF I MARRY RICH, I CAN HAVE THE LIFE I WANT.

YOU COULD ALSO WORK REALLY HARD AND EARN IT YOURSELF.

JO, I DON'T WANT TO FIGHT ABOUT THIS. OKAY? LET'S JUST HAVE A GOOD TIME.

THIS IS GOING TO BE THE *BEST NIGHT OF YOUR LIFE!*

I DIDN'T WANT TO GO WITH YOU ANYWAY.

I LIKE BEING BY MYSELF.

A BUNCH.

SO THERE.

HEY.

YOU, *UH*, WANNA DANCE?

SORRY, I GOTTA GO!

FROM: Josephine March
TO: Robert March
SENT: January 3

Hey-hey Dad!

It's a new year now, and everything feels different and yet somehow the same. Amy is still the family baby and the life of the party. Beth is still quiet and shy, and a true connoisseur of fine music. Meg is still obsessed with fashion and marrying rich. (Don't tell her I said that.) And Mom still works too hard and misses you every day. Same as the rest of us.

While I don't agree with war, I understand your desire to protect your family and country. But I wish you could just come home already. Of course, if I were making wishes, I would wish for a utopia where the world is at peace. Then we could all create art and live in harmony and all people would be free to be themselves. That must sound naive. But since I'm only sixteen, I am granting myself a few more years of remaining blissfully optimistic.

After all, I've lived something of a charmed life. My biological father left Mom and me before I turned two. And when I was four, Mom met you. I remember the first time I met you and Meg. As we walked up to that diner, Mom's hands were so sweaty. She said to me, "Please, please behave. I really like Robert." When we got to the diner, I didn't know what to expect. Mom had already told me you were black, which was funny to me, because I didn't see how that mattered.

When you saw Mom, your face lit up. I could tell you liked Mom as much as she liked you. Then you turned to me. You bent down on your knee, looked me in the eye, and shook my hand. "I heard you like books," you said. Then you handed me *Alice in Wonderland*. (The original one with the Sir John Tenniel illustrations, which is the best one, of course.) And you added, "I hope we can be friends."

And somehow—perhaps a child's intuition—I knew. You weren't like my birth father, who left. You were a good man. So I wrapped my arms around your neck and said, "Silly bear, we already are friends."

The day would have been perfect if it had ended there. Instead, Meg pulled my hair, and I started crying. Ha! Mom looked like she was going to have a heart attack. You just smiled that warm smile of yours and said, "They're already acting like sisters." And we were. And we still are. Except it's not acting. We still fight, but I love Meg. I am the luckiest girl on the planet to have the family that I do. I know that. Well, most of the time anyways. But on days when I want to scream or throw things, I take a deep breath and remember one of my happiest memories....

After the wedding, with Mom still in her dress and you in your tux, you bent your knee and said: "My last name is March. That means I'm a March. So is Meg, and so is your mom too now. How would you feel if I adopted you, so you could have my last name too? How would you feel about being my daughter?"

No one had ever given me a choice like that. I mean, my own father wanted nothing to do with me. He left me and Mom without a second thought. But you? You could have ignored me, or treated me like a fairy-tale stepchild, or just let things stay as they were. But you were different. You wanted me to feel loved. You wanted me to feel like I belonged. I will always remember the day, how proud I was when we went to the courthouse, and how I got to tell the judge I wanted to change my last name because I was a March.

I love you, Dad.

P.S. I love this photo of us...

P.P.S. A quote I found just for you...

"I believe that what we become depends on what our fathers teach us at odd moments, when they aren't trying to teach us. We are formed by little scraps of wisdom."

—Umberto Eco,
Foucault's Pendulum

CHAPTER 4

Back to the Grind...

...DOES THAT MAKE SENSE?

YES, MISS MEG.

WHO WANTS BROWN RICE AND BROCCOLI FOR DINNER?

CAN'T WE HAVE PIZZA?

SORRY, YOU KNOW I HAVE TO FOLLOW YOUR MOM'S RULES.

YUCK.

DOUBLE YUCK.

...AND THE PRINCESS WAITED AND WAITED AND WAITED, WAITING FOR HER WEALTHY PRINCE TO COME RESCUE HER FROM HER HORRIBLE JOB. BUT HE TOOK HIS SWEET TIME.

THAT'S NOT HOW THE STORY GOES!

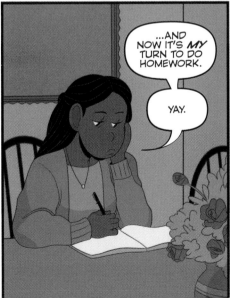

...AND NOW IT'S *MY* TURN TO DO HOMEWORK.

YAY.

GIRLS, YOU KNOW THE RULES.

ROUND 1: TALK ABOUT WHAT'S BOTHERING YOU. TAKE A BITE.

ROUND 2: COME UP WITH A SOLUTION. TAKE A BITE.

ROUND 3: NAME SOMETHING YOU'RE GRATEFUL FOR. TAKE A BITE.

YOU WANT TO START, AMY?

NO.

OW! THAT HURTS.

GIMME ICE CREAM.

NOPE. YOU KNOW THE RULES.

YOU MUST *SHARE* TO TASTE OF THE MAGIC TREAT.

I'LL GO FIRST. SOMETIMES IT'S HARD TO TUTOR AND SIT FOR THE KING FAMILY BECAUSE THEY'RE SO RICH.

IT MAKES ME JEALOUS. THEN I FEEL BAD FOR BEING JEALOUS.

WORKING FOR AUNT CATH IS HARD. SHE'S CRITICAL ABOUT EVERYTHING. NOTHING I DO IS RIGHT. IT'S EXHAUSTING.

NO MATTER HOW MUCH I DUST AND VACUUM AND CLEAN, THERE'S MORE TO DUST AND VACUUM AND CLEAN. IT'S NEVER-ENDING.

I LIKE THE WAY I DRESS!

FROM: Beth March
TO: Robert March
SENT: January 28

Hi Daddy!

How are you? I am fine. Middle school is fun. The kids are okay, but the classes are real fun. Did I tell you we have something called electives— that means classes we get to choose. And I chose music! We get to play different instruments. I thought I would like the piano or maybe the flute more, but it turns out I really like playing guitar.

Oh, and Jo found this old vintage record store in Bushwick. She took me there and bought me two records. I chose The Ronettes and Ella Fitzgerald. I love old music! When you're back, can I play them for you? I bet you and Mom would like to dance to them.

I miss you a whole whole bunch. Don't tell my sisters, but I still sleep with Mr. Furry Burry, the bear you brought me back from Kabul when I was little. He kinda smells and he's missing an eye, but he reminds me of you. (I included a pic for you!)

Come home soon—and safe!
Love you forever, Beth!

B *I* U

Send

CHAPTER 5

Neighbors

FROM: Amy March
TO: Robert March
SENT: Feb 21

daddy!

meg & jo & beth said i should email u, so i am. i would write u more, but i hate writing cause it feels like HOMEWOKR. yuck! i rather talk to u on the phone. or skype!

i hope u come home soon. i know u miss me so here are pics of me ebing awesome!

Send

XOXOXOXOXOX
OXOXOXOXOXO
XOXOXOXOXOX
OXOXOXOXOXO
XOXOXOXOXOX
OXOXOXOXOXO,
your FAVE
daughter, AMY!

CHAPTER 6

The Gift of Music

FROM: Beth March
TO: Robert March
SENT: March 22

Oh Dad! The most wonderful thing happened—I got a guitar! Mr. Marquez from across the street gave it to me. Mom tried to talk him out of it, but he insisted. He heard me playing and says I have real talent. Do you think it's possible? Meg loves clothes and Jo loves books and Amy loves art (and video games). And I love music so much, but it scares me to death to play in front of others. Jo said that shouldn't stop me. She told me that some of the best musicians just write the songs. They don't have to get up on stage and play in front of anybody. They just get to make music and sell it to other people. I think that's what I want to be when I grow up—a songwriter.

There's just something about music. It comes from deep inside, from that special place in a soul that connects with everyone else. Some songs make me want to dance or cry or laugh or hug Mom. It's amazing how a few words and an instrument can do that. Every song, no matter what it is, makes everyone feel something. People either love it or hate it. (I mean I guess some people might just like it, but even liking something is a feeling.) And I want to make that kind of music.

Now I just have to decide what kind of music I like most. Pop? (Maybe.) Country? (I don't know if I'd be good at that.) Rap? (Definitely not!) Haha. I asked Meg what she thought, and she said I should make the kind of music I want to hear. But I like so much! I like Beyoncé and Stevie Wonder and Stevie Nicks and Dolly Parton and Nina Simone and Prince and Tina Turner and Joni Mitchell and Alicia Keys and The Temptations and Norah Jones and those are just my favorites!

I don't know where to begin....Actually, this email just gave me an idea. I think I'll write a song about YOU. I miss you Daddy.

Love you love you love you.
Yours, Beth

CHAPTER 7

Hell Hath No Fury Like a Sister Scorned...

April 4

I'm a horrible person. A monster.

No, I mean it. I've been so mad at Amy, and today—today she almost died. We had gone to the museum and she stepped in front of a bus. I was so scared. It's like her whole life flashed before my eyes. I know it sounds like a cliché, but that's what happened. I remembered when she was a bump in Mom's tummy. I remembered when she was born, and how tiny her fingers were, and when they squeezed mine. I remembered changing her dirty diapers. I remembered the first time she had a bad dream and crawled into bed with me because Meg was at Kennedy's. I remembered everything. And I froze.

The bus would have hit her. It would have—I can't even write it. But Meg saved her. Like some kind of superhero, Meg moved faster than I could have imagined and she pulled Amy back. Two feet. Twenty-four inches. That's all that stood between Amy and

Sorry. I had to stop writing for a minute. I can't stop crying. Mom told me not to be hard on myself, but I should have been the one to save her. I was closest. Yet fear got the better of me. I pray there's never a next time. But if there is, I'll move. Mind over matter, I'll force my body to act, to be a hero.

It was such a powerful moment. One I don't think I'll ever forget. When it was over, I sat on the steps of the museum thinking about the whole of life, and how it can all just be taken away in a split second. Who knows how much time any of us has on this big silly planet, but I plan to take full advantage. If I could just get over my fears of what everyone will think if they knew the real me...if they knew my secret...

CHAPTER 8

School Drama...

YOU BETTER NOT TELL ON ME! OR I'LL DO EVEN WORSE!

WHAT'S GOING ON OVER THERE?!

I DIDN'T DO ANYTHING, MRS. BIRD! I SWEAR!

AMY MARCH, PLEASE TELL ME WHAT HAPPENED.

NOTHING HAPPENED. I FELL DOWN. SORRY.

FROM: Amy March
TO: Robert March
SENT: April 18

hi Daddy!

meg and jo say i should write u more, so that's what i'm doing. i dont know what to rite about so i guess i will tell you about my week, which was kinda crazy. this girl tara connor is awful to me all the time, makes fun of my hair and my skin and especially my nose, which is pretty dumb because i like my nose. i mean i guess sometimes i dont but that's because tara made fun of it so much, it made me so mad, but i didnt want to fight her or anything because i thought i'd probably get in more trouble than her, cuz she's white and i'm black, and thats what happens. my teacher mrs nelson makes us read news articles cuz she says its important to know whats happening in the world and its always in the news that black people are getting hurt or worse by people in our country, like cops and other people too. it makes me really sad. but mrs nelson says the world is getting better, too slowly she says, but i think slow is better than not moving forward at all, right? mrs nelson is teaching about the civil war which is really intresting cuz it ended the confedrcy (the south), and abolished slavery and freed 4 million slaves.

its weird to think we might have been related to slaves, and we probably were because we are from here and not from africa, which is one of the mean names tara always called me. but mom says i shouldnt be insulted cuz Africa is a beautiful place and all people are beautiful no matter

Send

where they from. anyways, she punched me, not mom, tara did, tara punched me right in the face and the only reason I didn't hit her back was because she is white, and I got really scared that if i hit her i would go to jail. but then meg and jo and mom figured out what happened and told the prinipcal, mrs vasquez who i've never met but turns out is really nice, and she called tara's mom, and boy did her head hit the roof! tara's mom was so mad! she dragged tara out of school in front of everyone and tara was crying cuz her mom is sending her to boarding school cuz she's so horrible. i would feel bad, but i dont. tara was mean to a lot of people not just me. anyway, it turns out mrs nelson who i thought was racist isn't racist at all. she says i'm one of her favorite students, and i'm glad cuz i think she's really nice! and she likes my art! she even told mom i should take art for my elective in middle school. of course mom got mad cuz i was drawing in history and told me i need to pay better attention. now that i like mrs. nelson i'll definitly try harder. probably not with science lessons tho. i hate science

wow! i wrote a lot, didn't i? coolio. i'm gonna go doodle and draw some before bed. love you daddy. come home already!
your FAVORITe daughter, AMY!

CHAPTER 9

Money and Freedom...

FROM: Megan March
TO: Robert March
SENT: May 18

Hi Dad,

I just wanted to tell you how proud I am of you and the sacrifices you're making for us. You never lose patience, never doubt, never complain, yet always manage to hope. You work hard, and you wait so cheerfully that I'm ashamed to admit that I have done otherwise. But I'm turning over a new leaf.

Starting today, I want to be more like you. I want to be stronger, kinder, and more patient. Not just with my sisters but with everyone. For some time now, I've been ashamed of being poor. But this weekend (in the Hamptons of all places!), I realized that I'm not. I'm rich in the only way that counts: I have a family that values and loves me.

I am the luckiest girl in the world. And I am proud to be your daughter.

I love you, always and forever,
Meg

CHAPTER 10

Dirty Dishes

FROM: Beth March
TO: Robert March
SENT: June 19

Hey Dad,

How are you? I am fine. School just ended and all of us sisters are going to enjoy our summer break. Though it would be better if you were here too. I'd love to go to the beach, just the two of us. I know that's selfish, but I want to play you a song on my guitar that I've been working on. I'm too embarrassed to play it for anyone else. But I would play it for you.

What else? Um, I don't know. I just woke up and it's almost noon. Please don't think I'm lazy, I'm really not! Lately, I've been getting bad headaches, and I'm really tired all the time. Jo says it's the heat from global warming. It is really hot here. Is it hot where you are?

Anyways, it's nice being out of school. I've been staying up late watching movies. Not bad ones! Just Disney princess ones. I know I'm too old for them, but I still like them. (Though I wish they had more black princesses.)

Okay, I'm going to go take a nap. Just kidding! (Or maybe I'm not.)

I miss you. Please come home soon.
Love you forever,
Beth

Jo's Journal: KEEP OUT

"Carpe diem. Seize the day, boys. Make your lives extraordinary."

I wish I had written that. But I can't take credit. Robin
Williams said it in that movie <u>Dead Poets Society</u>. I admit
that I've watched it FOUR times this summer, but I can't
help it. It hits me on so many levels. And it's so true.
Seize the day! Because who knows, it could be your last.
(Yeesh. Morbid much?)

I don't mean to be, but it's true. Life flies by. Take this
summer, for instance. It's already the end of June. Summer
only just began, and the first month is almost done and gone.
The last two weeks have flown by as if nothing more than an
orange leaf on an autumn wind, a fall that is just around the
corner.

That's why I'm trying to read one book a week this summer.
So far I've read <u>The Color Purple</u> by Alice Walker (and cried
through most of it) and <u>The Hours</u> by Michael Cunningham.
Both are heartbreaking and beautiful and so wonderful, and
I only hope that one day I can write so exquisitely. But there
is this thing that worries me...

After I read a great book, I am left wanting more. It takes
every effort not to turn the last page and start again on the
first. (I mean, if I read every book I loved over and over, I'd
never get to the next.) So instead, I go online and look up
what I can about the author. I want to know what inspired
them, what moved them to craft such wonderful words

and perfect vernacular. And do you know what I've found? They've all endured some horrible, tragic circumstance that forever changed them. And it terrifies me.

Why? Because on one hand, I want to write beautifully, but I don't want to suffer to do it. On the other hand, it makes me feel as though I am overdue for some terrible event.

Yikes. I just got goose pimples all over my body. I am thoroughly freaking myself out. I do want to write, and I want to write well, and I want to win the Pulitzer for fiction one day, which is kind of ridiculous because there are so many amazing writers out there and who am I? I mean, I don't want to be famous, and I don't want to be rich (though I wouldn't complain about that), but ultimately, I just want to be recognized as worthy....

That's it, isn't it? I want to be worthy. Because right now, with my... secret... I don't feel worthy. I feel dishonest. I feel like a liar, a charlatan, a con artist. I suppose, in my own way, I am suffering. But it's not as though I can't breathe each day. Our world has changed. People—society—they're more tolerant than ever. Heck, just a few decades ago, Mom and Dad wouldn't have been able to get married. Now, they're celebrated. And I want to be celebrated too. But I don't have the courage to say the words. I don't know what I'm scared of... that Mom and Dad won't love me anymore. That Meg and Beth and Amy will look at me different. I don't think they would, but what if? What if it bothers them? What if they hate me? I can't bear the thought of that. So I don't say anything.

So I guess my point is, if I can't be me, if I can't be celebrated... then maybe (at the very least) my writing can.

I shouldn't feel sorry for myself. I have a good life. I have two parents who love me, three sisters who have my back, friends who I can tell anything to.... Well, almost anything. See? I am happy. And what does a happy person have to write about? Nothing!

Ugh. There goes that feeling again! That sense that something terrible is coming, something that will test me, some awful personal tragedy. I don't know what it is, and that terrifies me. I like my life as it is. I don't want it to change. But change is constant. And I guess all of us have to face something sooner or later. So carpe diem!

In that vein, I'll end this entry with my second favorite quote from Dead Poet's Society...

> KEATING: "Seize the day. Gather ye rosebuds while ye may." Why does the writer use these lines?

> CHARLIE: Because he's in a hurry.

> KEATING: No. Ding! Thank you for playing anyway. Because we are food for worms, lads. Because, believe it or not, each and every one of us in this room is one day going to stop breathing, turn cold and die.

Me? Josephine March? I'm not ready to die. Not even close. No worm food for me, not yet! I have more to write. So much more...

CHAPTER 11

Fireworks

July 4

Laurie has ruined everything! I'm so upset, and I don't know what to do. I think I've just lost my best friend. Okay, deep breaths, like Mom says. Writing will calm me down. Let me start at the beginning...

Today began so perfectly. We Skyped with Dad, and each of us got to speak with him for as long as we wanted. Then Mom and Mr. Marquez and our neighbors had a block party to celebrate the 4th of July. Mr. Chang cooked all day at the grill so people could have as many burgers and hot dogs as they wanted. The Rodriguez family made homemade tamales and seven-layer bean dip. And Mr. Bernstein even brought out a karaoke machine. We ate and we sang and we laughed and we danced, and everything was just so perfect...

Then we all went to the roof to watch the fireworks. We were having a great time until we started talking about our futures. Meg got all preachy and started talking about family and doing what they want us to. Okay, so that's not exactly what she said, but that's what I heard, because...well, you know. Of course, rather than deal with my own stuff, I started screaming at Meg. I just got so mad, because I can't be me...the real me. I know... real mature, right?

Meanwhile, Laurie thought I was sticking up for him. Telling him he should live his own life and not care what his family thinks. Me and my stupid mouth...I wish I could take my own advice. I'm such a hypocrite. So yeah, that's when Laurie had to go and kiss me!

That kiss could destroy our friendship. What was he thinking?!
Why did he have to kiss me? Why couldn't he have kissed Meg?
Or someone who wanted it? Instead, he had to go and kiss me.
And what did I do? I ran away! Of course I ran away. He's one
of my closest friends—my best friend (if I don't count Meg).
I don't want to lose that. And now how am I supposed to face
him?!

I just don't know why he would do that. I certainly didn't lead him
to the conclusion that that's what I wanted. I don't flirt. I don't
dress like a girl. I don't even let him open doors for me. Maybe it's
true what they say: Guys only want what they can't have.

Ugh. Maybe I am to blame. After all, I'm the one keeping
secrets. Not just from my family and friends, but from myself.
I know who and what I really am, but I'm not ready to face it.
So what I viewed as a friendship, maybe Laurie assumed was
something more. I wish I could go along with it. After all, Laurie
would be a wonderful partner. He's lovely and funny and smart
and we both like to read. But for me, the magic spark just isn't
there, not like the chemistry I feel when...

God. I am such a coward. I can't even write it. It's like being
afraid of my own shadow. But this is the world we live in, one in
which not all men and women are created equal. People are still
prejudiced against others, whether for the color of their skin,
the shape of their bodies, the beliefs in their gods, or the love in
their hearts. Why can't everyone just accept everyone for who
they are?

I want to tell Laurie the truth, but I'm scared to, just like I'm
scared to tell my family. Maybe one day...but not today.

CHAPTER 12

Good News, Bad News...

July 27

I feel so helpless. Jo said I should channel my feelings. She suggested a punching bag or running, but I hate exercise. So I thought I'd do what she does, and write down what I'm feeling. Maybe it'll help. It certainly couldn't make me feel worse. I've never felt so horrible in my whole life.

Dad is hurt and on the other side of the world. Mom says there was a stray blast, and he got caught in it. The doctors wouldn't tell her how bad it was on the phone, only that he lost one of his legs, and that they're doing everything they can. They are moving him from the Middle East to a hospital in Germany. That's where Mom is heading right now.

I can't imagine what Dad must be going through. I'm almost grateful he's in a coma. But does he feel pain? Is he dreaming? Is he thinking of his family? Is he going to be okay? I wish I could go be with him too. All I want is to hold his hand and let him know he'll get better. But will he?

I feel so lost. Like the whole world took a wrong turn. How could this happen to my dad? We all know military service is dangerous, but it didn't seem real until the phone rang and Mom collapsed. Then suddenly it was all too real. And there's nothing I can do. Why isn't there anything I can do?!

Maybe...maybe...I should ask myself, what would Dad do? What would he want me to do? That's easy. He'd want me to stay strong and take care of my sisters. So that's what I'll do. That's all I can do...

I love you, Daddy. Please come home.

Meg

CHAPTER 13

Words Across the World...

FROM: Josephine March
TO: Madison March
SENT: August 26

Hey Mom,

I tried Skyping you but forgot about the time difference over there. You probably fell asleep in Dad's room again. No worries. But call when you can. I know hearing your voice would help everyone over here. We're staying strong, like you asked, but we miss you both every day.

Everything is good on this end. School started this week, and I like my teachers. Well, except Mr. Tucker. He's my chemistry teacher and I don't understand half the words coming out of his mouth. But my English teacher, Mrs. Humphrey, might be the best teacher I've ever had. She also teaches an elective class called Literature and World Culture. It sounds like a college course, right? I can't wait to take it next semester.

As for everyone else, we're all okay. Meg has been a total boss. She's practically taken your place, making sure everyone gets fed and brushes their teeth before bed. She won't even let me watch TV after ten! But she's been so good about juggling her own job and taking care of our family.

Amy is…well, Amy. Like they said in the 1920s, she's full of "piss and vinegar." That one is so full of life, she's like a juggernaut of energy. But if nothing else, she keeps all of us laughing.

I am a little worried about Beth. Her appetite isn't what it used to be, and she wants to sleep all the time. I think she's taking the news about Dad's leg the hardest. She did pick up her guitar tonight and start playing, but she chose such a melancholy song and went to bed after. Meg and I will make sure to give her extra attention this weekend and see if we can snap her out of it.

We love you so very very very much. My fingers are crossed you can both come home soon.
Love, Jo

FROM: Megan March
TO: Robert March
SENT: August 30

Dad!

You're awake! I'm so happy and grateful and just over-the-moon happy to know you're on the mend. When we Skype Mom, we always hope for good news. But tonight, when she said, "There's someone who wants to speak to you," my heart swelled so big I thought it would burst. Seeing your smile again made everything right in the world.

I know we only just finished speaking, but Amy was hogging the whole conversation. So I thought I'd write to say how relieved I am that you're awake. I can't imagine what you've been through. Or what you are about to go through. But Mom says she is friends with everyone in the physical therapy department at the hospital and you'll be in good hands when you get home. The next few months are going to be hard, but you have Mom with you now, and all of us at home, praying for your quick recovery. Come home soon.

We love you so very much. Can't wait to see you. —Meg

Send

FROM: Amy March
TO: Robert March
SENT: August 31

Daddy!

Meg said I could only get on the computer if I emailed you, which is what I was going to do anyways. She thinks I only get on here to look at Youtube clips, which is maybe usually kinda true, but not today, cuz I made you some pictures. I'm really talented, I know. I was going to mail them to you, but Jo said they'll take forever in snail mail, and you'll probably be home before then, right?

How are u? I miss you! What's new? Besides your leg? Beth seems freaked out about your leg, but I'm not. I think it's cool. You should get a robot leg, like Cyborg from Justice League. Or maybe an animal leg. If I could have any animal leg, I'd probably get a cheetah, cuz its fast. I love u a whole bunch but I'm tired of writing now so I'm going to do more art and watch TV. Come home fast!

Love u 4-ever. Ur fave girl, Amy

Send

CHAPTER 14

The Doctor Is In...

FROM: Megan March
TO: Esther March
SENT: September 10

Hi Gammy,

Thanks for calling me last night. I'm sorry I cried the whole time. I just couldn't keep it in. It's like, most of the time, I can hold it together, and be strong—for Beth, for Dad, for Mom—but when I heard your voice, the floodgates opened. I know you say I can always be myself with you, and I guess that *was* me being myself. I really needed that cry.

I've been trying to be so strong for everyone, and I think I have been. But all of it is wearing me down. I'm tired and exhausted and there's still so much to do. I wake up and pick up the house. Then, I go to school and try to concentrate, which is practically impossible. Then, I go to the hospital, so Mom can go home and take a shower, or I bring her clothes and food. And some nights, I still have to go to the Kings' to watch their kids when all I want to be doing is staying at Beth's side. And after all that, there's still homework left to do. The worst part is—nothing seems as important right now as spending time with Beth or with Dad. And he's on the other side of the planet.

But I'm glad you're there with him now. It was good to talk to him tonight too. But I can't cry with him the way I do with you. I'm his firstborn, and I don't want him to think I'm weak. I feel like I'm letting everyone down, even though you keep saying I'm not.

That thing you said on the phone, about staying in the present moment, it struck a chord with me. And that quote: "This too shall pass." It helps remembering that. Every time I feel a wave of stress coming at me, I say it, and take a deep breath. It seems to be helping. Somehow, you always know the right thing to say. Thank you for being there, Gammy. I don't know what we'd do without you.

Give my love to Dad. And I'll give your love to Beth. —Meg

P.S. Thank you for keeping my secret about my boyfriend. I don't think my sisters could understand me dating someone right now, but Brooks is the only thing that helps me forget the pain. He's handsome and charming, and he's been so wonderfully supportive through the last few months. I can't wait for you to meet him when everything gets better…

Jo's Journal: KEEP OUT

Everything is falling apart. And it's not fair. How much is one family supposed to bear? How much more can we take? My father is hurt and unable to come home. My little sister has cancer and the chemo seems to take more and more away from her with each treatment. And at the end of every long day, I lie down to go to sleep, and I can't. I lie there, wide awake, wondering if I'll see Beth tomorrow.

I know it's morbid and horrible, but I can't control my thoughts. I want her to get better, for everything to go back to the way it was before the whole world crashed down around our ears. But there's nothing I can do. I can't control this. I can't fix it. I can't punch or scream at cancer. It makes the mightiest of men into mice. I am trying to trust in modern medicine and the doctors and the hospital staff, but every time I go there, I want to know why people aren't doing more. We live in the 21st century—how can we not have a cure for cancer yet? We can talk instantaneously to people on the other side of the globe and we can fly to the moon and send satellites to the far reaches of space—so why don't we have a cure for disease?

Why does life have to be this hard? At least for kids. Beth is an innocent. She shouldn't have to suffer this. If I could, I would take her pain. I would. But I can't. All I can do is write, letting my words be a prayer, a plea to God or Jesus or Allah or Buddha or whoever is up there, hoping that my words sway their hearts and let me keep my sister—even if for just another day...

CHAPTER 15

The Falling of Leaves...

Jo's Journal: KEEP OUT

Change is good. It's necessary. Sometimes I forget that and try to cling to how things are. But then autumn comes and the leaves fall off the trees, and everywhere I go, I see green has turned to orange and brown, and fallen away to reveal something beneath....It doesn't mean things are ending, just changing.

Tonight, as I was getting ready for bed, I found myself staring into the mirror, not recognizing myself—but in the best possible way.

I don't have any hair anymore. A few days ago, I shaved my head. For Beth. The chemo is making her hair fall out, and I can tell it's upsetting her. Right now, she needs to have a positive outlook on life. But how can she do that when the chemo that's killing the cancer is making her sick? I felt so powerless, and I wanted to help, but I didn't know how. Then it just occurred to me:

Like the leaves falling outside, what if I cut my hair? Maybe if I shaved my head, Beth wouldn't feel so alone. Then Meg did it too. So did Amy. And when Beth saw—it's like the fear drained away from her eyes. The four of us are sisters. We always have been, and we always will be. I think the cancer made Beth feel like she was different. But now that we all have the same haircut? That worry is gone. I only pray it helps her recovery.

So yeah. Josephine March is bald. I know guys shave their heads all the time, but for a girl it's different. After I did it, for a minute I was like, in total shock. But almost instantly, I was okay. I kinda love it. I'm excited to see what I look like with a crew cut. Or maybe a pixie cut. Either way, I don't want to grow it out long again. This feels right. I feel more like... me. Like I'm closer to the real version of myself.

Me aside, I'm really proud of Meg. I wanted to ask her, but I never thought she would even consider it—not in a million years! Meg loves fashion and beauty and worries what others think about her. Cutting her hair meant sacrificing something that she considered beautiful and feminine and important to her appearance. By shaving it off, I think she learned that she doesn't have to rely on other's perceptions of herself to feel validated. In a way, I think what she did makes her even braver than me. Not to mention that it is so hard and takes so long for a woman to grow her hair out long and healthy. Good for Meg.

And she's not the only one. Amy is learning to be more self-aware, maybe even modest. I think that it shows she's becoming more empathetic—not that she wasn't already. Of course, every day, she calls us from Aunt Cath's when she's getting ready and says, "Where will I put my barrettes? Should I glue them to the side of my head?" Hahaha. That girl is crazy. But I love her. I love all my sisters.

Yes, it's autumn now, and the leaves will fall, and winter will come, and things will change. But I know we'll come out the other side of this stronger.

CHAPTER 16

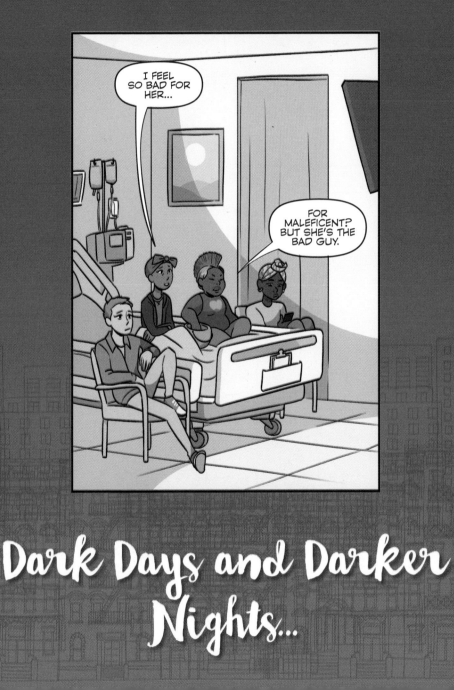

Dark Days and Darker Nights...

FROM: Megan March
TO: Robert March
SENT: November 1

Hi Dad,

I'm sorry I didn't get a chance to call last night. We were staying with Beth at the hospital for Halloween and it got too late. I didn't want to wake you. But I promise I'll call today when I get home from school.

This autumn feels so strange. Usually I don't even notice the changing of the leaves or the shortening of the days. But this year, everything feels so sad. You know it's tradition for us to go trick or treating and then watch a scary movie. But this year Beth asked if we could do Disney movies instead. I don't mind, but it just felt so odd, us trying to watch movies while Beth battles cancer and you recover from your injuries.

When are you coming home? We really miss you.
I really miss you.

Your daughter, forever and always, Meg

Send

FROM: Amy March
TO: Robert March
SENT: November 1

Heya Daddy,

Beth is still sick. And everyone is sad. And we miss you.
I know your legs won't be the same, but I don't care.
Please come home soon. Please?

—Amy

Send

November 7

I've never been so afraid.

I think Beth is dying.

I don't know how long I have left with her, so I refuse to leave her side. Mom and Meg tried to get me to go home, but I refused. I know they understand. We're all going through this together, but it's Beth. My Beth. She is more than my sister. She's my best friend, my kindred spirit. She's my favorite. I know we're not supposed to have favorite sisters, but I do. Beth is like me. She is a creator, of words, and music, and...

I'm afraid that her song is over.

Tonight I looked at her, lying there, pale and gaunt, like a ghost of her former self. And I thought, this is it. I kissed her and I said my goodbyes.

Please don't let this be it.

I want to be hopeful, like the others, but I can't. The rest of my family has faith, but if I'm being honest...I don't think I do. Our world is a terrible and dark place. If it weren't, then how do you explain innocent children getting sick?

It's not fair. It's not!

This life feels unbearable right now. Like I can't breathe. I wish I could change places with Beth. I would in an instant. My life for hers. If only it were that simple.

I love you, Beth.

I love you so much.

And if this is our last night together....I only hope that I will see you again. Perhaps on the other side...

November 14

Jo's Journal: KEEP OUT

Beth is going to be okay. At least I think she is. I was never that good at science. But I think I understand some of this stuff now.

When leukemia gets diagnosed, there are about 100 billion cancer cells in the body. (Can you even imagine?). During the first part of treatment (called Induction), they try to kill 99.9% of the leukemia cells. That's enough to achieve "Remission." But that still leaves about 100 million cancer cells in the body. These also have to be destroyed. So the next phase is called Consolidation. That lasts about one to two months. And it's really really intense. That's why Beth had to stay at the hospital, so she didn't get a serious infection or in case of complications. But she came through. Like a total champ!

The last couple of months have been exhausting for everyone, but Dr. Shah says now is where the real work begins. We have about two years of maintenance chemotherapy ahead of us. The goal is to destroy the remaining cancer cells. Two years seems like a lifetime, but if it'll help Beth, then I'll do it. We all will.

Bring it on, life. March girls can take anything you throw at us.

CHAPTER 17

Colder and Warmer...

KNOCK
KNOCK

HEY.

SO...
UH...

...YOU
WANNA
GO FOR A
WALK?

SURE.

November 20

Meg is a liar!

Laurie and I were in the park, and I saw her...with Brooks. Laurie told me they've been dating for months. MONTHS! I guess it started just after they met at the 4th of July party we had. Meg's been so secretive and annoying with her texts and calls, and I was certain it was just Kennedy, but now I know the truth. I can't believe Meg would lie to me. I mean, no, I guess she didn't LIE-lie, but she withheld the truth, which is practically the same thing. If I was dating someone, I would tell her. But here she is, keeping a secret—a huge secret.

I should confront Meg, but I want to give her the chance to tell me. Though it's already been two days since I saw her in the park, and not a word! Brooks was on his knee, her hand in his. I think we all know what that means, what he asked her. They're engaged! Meg is going to be married! It's ridiculous. This isn't 1868. She hasn't even finished high school! Mom and Dad are going to FLIP OUT when they find out.

I am furious. Meg isn't just my sister, she's my best friend. Why wouldn't she tell me that she and Brooks were seeing each other? I mean, if she loves him, why be ashamed of it? He's exactly what she always wanted: handsome, educated, RICH. According to Laurie, he's a trust fund kid with a work ethic. That's a modern-day Prince Charming if I've ever heard of one. Of course, Meg would say yes. I can't believe she's getting married! She's going to skip college to be some stupid bride and probably have kids and…OMG. I'm going to be an aunt before I finish high school.

Meg is making a huge mistake. She has her whole life ahead of her, and she has so much potential that she'll waste if she gets married before she finds out who she really is.…I don't know what to do. Should I tell Mom? Should I keep quiet? UGH. I hate secrets!!! And yes, I understand the complete and total irony of ME, of all people, loathing secrets. I may be a hypocrite, but at least I'm not some child bride like Meg!

CHAPTER 18

Giving Thanks...

December 1

My name is Jo March, and I am gay.

I can't believe I just wrote that. I've thought it a million times, but I've never put it down on paper. I was too scared to. But then at Thanksgiving, there was all this drama (my fault), and it just came out. The words, I mean. But then so did I. I came out to my sisters and Mom. And they were fine with it. They didn't even care. Later, Mom admitted that she suspected, but she never wanted to press it. She wanted me to figure it out for myself. Beth and Amy said they knew. Really, only Meg was surprised. But she pointed out that my lack of fashion sense should have been an indicator—which I quickly busted her for being a stereotype! Silly Meg. She apologized like a hundred times for saying it.

Of course, no sooner had I come out than Dad came home. It turns out Mr. Marquez paid for him (and Gammy!) to fly home first-class. He said a family should be together for the holidays. It was so sweet of him. Though if you ask me, he did it because he has a crush on Gammy Esther. They spent the rest of the evening sipping wine in the corner while the rest of us caught up.

The day after Thanksgiving, I pulled Dad aside so I could tell him my own news. At first, he was really quiet. I've heard so many horrible coming-out stories that I started to grow anxious he was going to disown me. Instead, he kissed my forehead and said, "At some point, you're going to encounter intolerance. When that happens, I want you to hold your head high and be proud of who you are. The world's gotten a lot better, but it still has a ways to go. Until then, know that you are never alone. You have me, and you have your family to back you up."

We hugged for a long time. Then he told me how the Black Panther Party were allies with the LGBTQ community in the 1970s. Both groups struggled to be recognized as equal to the rest of the populace. Jean Genet, a famous French gay writer and activist, became friends with David Hilliard, Black Panther chief of staff. They toured the U.S., traveling state to state, speaking to promote tolerance. I had no idea.

Looks like Dad still has some things to teach me. ☺

There's only one person I need to reach: Aunt Cath. She disappeared after I came out. I called and left messages but she hasn't returned them. She only sent me a text saying to take the month of December off to reconnect with my dad. I asked Mom if Aunt Cath was maybe homophobic, and Mom didn't say anything except that she loved me and so did Aunt Cath. I don't know why, but it really bothers me that Aunt Cath would react like this. I thought we were closer than that...But I won't stop trying. She'll come around. Won't she?

But Dad is home! I can hardly believe it. It makes home feel like...well, home again. With Beth getting better day by day, and Dad in physical therapy for his leg, it's like everything is on the mend. We're all healing, physically, mentally, and spiritually. And now that we're all together, I am certain we will heal a lot faster.

FROM: Beth March
TO: Alejandro Marquez
SENT: December 4

Dear Mr. Marquez,

I wanted to thank you again for everything you've done for me this year. All the flowers you sent while I was in the hospital were nice. And Gammy Esther told me you paid for her and Dad to come home in time for Thanksgiving. And of course, you gave me my guitar. (I named him Mr. Strings.)

Now that I'm feeling better, I've been playing Mr. Strings every day. I've written two new songs. And I am playing in my school's holiday talent show. Six months ago, I would have never played in front of anybody. But after fighting cancer, things don't seem quite as scary.

Anyways, that is the reason I am writing. I would like you to see me play. Would you like to come to the holiday talent show?

The information is below.

Sincerely,
Beth

December 6

Dear Diary, it's me, Meg. Duh.

Life has been so crazy lately and I feel I have to write it down before I burst into tears.

First, Dad is home—which is wonderful. I couldn't be happier. Second, Beth is getting stronger every day. Again, more good news. Third, Jo is gay. Ever since she came out, she seems lighter, able to breathe and smile more easily. I'm pleased for her...and also a little jealous.

I didn't go to war, or have cancer, or feel like I had to hide a secret from the world. So why am I so confused?

Today, I had an interview at _Vogue_. I mean, that's a dream job for any girl who has ever liked fashion. A year ago, I would have killed for this meeting. Then last week, Brooks's mom made a call and got it for me, just like that. But when I was there, all

I thought about was Dad and about Beth...about the doctors who saved their lives. And I thought, fashion is wonderful, and it's art, and I love it, but I want to use my life to make a bigger difference. I think I want to be a lawyer.

Crazy, right? I'd never thought about it until I was sitting there in that interview. Maybe I've never admitted it to myself because of my obsession with being rich or taken care of. Or maybe because I didn't believe in myself enough to think I could do it. But after this last year? I feel like I'm stronger than I realized. And I don't want a job because my boyfriend's mom made a call. I want to earn it myself. But I guess that brings me to the next thing...

Brooks is wonderful. He's everything I've ever dreamed of in a man. He is handsome and charming and dresses well. He has ambition and wants to do good in the world. And yes, he comes from money, which doesn't hurt. He's perfect! In my head, he is the perfect catch. But in my heart...I'm not sure how I feel about him. I really really really like Brooks. But I'm not sure I love him.

A hundred years ago, a girl didn't have a lot of choices. She could either get married or be a spinster. She'd probably only know one or two eligible bachelors, and would have to just settle and make it work with whichever man chose her. Options were limited. But now? Now a woman can do anything. She can become an explorer, or a doctor, or a politician. She can be an editor or a model or a designer. She can fly to the moon, or become a teacher, or be a stay-at-home mom. There's no limit to what we can do.

After everything that's happened this year—with Dad, with Beth, with life—I'm just not sure I'm ready to settle...for either a job or a partner. I think I need to take some time to figure things out—to sort out what is best for me. And I think I know where to start...

Dear Santa,

Amy March here. U probly know this, but last year I stopped believing in you. Well, this year I changed my mind. Lots of good stuff happened, so I decided miracles are reel. And what's more miracle-u-lus (I don't know how to spell good) than a fat guy who flys all over the world and gives free presentz?

Anywaze, I wanted to tell you what I want for X-mas:

* Make ~~Physikal~~ Physical Therapy easier for Dad. He says its no fun.

* Help Beth to get totally better. No cancer! Also, get her some guitar picks—the kind with glitter in them.

* Get Meg some new lipstick and make-up. (She doesn't know I used hers to finish an art project.)

* Jo likes books so get her those.

* Mom needs a vacation! Maybe help her win a contest to a tropical island for her and Dad.

* Aunt Cath needs a vacation too.

* Get Gammy Esther a new house, one close to us. I think she would like to live nearby.

* Oh, and make sure every kid gets a present. I know some kid's families are poor and can't afford stuff. So make sure you take care of those ones first.

That's it! If you're wondering bout me, I don't need anything. I have ~~everyting~~ everything I need.

Thx, dude! —Amy

CHAPTER 19

Songs and Secrets...

FROM: Madison March
TO: Alejandro Marquez, Laurie Marquez, Gammy Esther, Cathleen Burroughs, Mr. Bernstein, Kennedy Gardiner… (click to show more)
SENT: December 20

HAPPY HOLIDAYS FROM THE MARCH FAMILY TO YOURS!

Send

CHAPTER 20

March of the Marches...

January 21

Today I marched with my sisters, both figuratively and literally. And while the world isn't where it should be, it's on its way...

Louisa May Alcott

was born on November 29, 1832, in Pennsylvania. She was the second of four daughters of educator and social reformer Amos Bronson Alcott and social worker Abigail May Alcott. Despite a great deal of moving from place to place, Alcott received a formal education from her father. Her early instruction was rounded out with lessons from family friends, such as influential intellectuals Henry David Thoreau, Ralph Waldo Emerson, Theodore Parker, Margaret Fuller, and Nathaniel Hawthorne, who is best known for having written *The Scarlet Letter*.

Her family lived in poverty, which made it necessary for Alcott to work at an early age. She made money working as a seamstress, a governess, a domestic helper, a teacher, and, of course, a writer.

In 1847, the Alcott home became a safe house for the Underground Railroad, a network of secret routes used by enslaved African Americans to escape from the South to free states in the North during the early nineteenth century. This was not the only cause Alcott would take up in her lifetime. She also looked to empower women, who at the time had few rights and could not vote. Eventually, she became the first woman to register to vote in Concord, Massachusetts, in a school board election. It was a small step but an important one.

The 1850s were a difficult time for the Alcotts. In 1858, her younger sister passed away and her older sister married. Alcott's sisterhood—which had meant so much to her—felt as though it were breaking apart. With little money and no work, Louisa May found herself filled with despair. It was during this time she found a biography of Charlotte Bronte, discovering many parallels to her own life. Soon after, Alcott began writing for *The Atlantic Monthly*.

When the American Civil War began, Alcott served as a nurse until she became deathly ill when she contracted typhoid. Her letters home during this time would soon bring her critical recognition as a writer. But it was in 1868 that Louisa May Alcott finally found great success when her novel *Little Women* was published. *Little Women* was a semiautobiographical story of her own childhood growing up with her sisters. It is on that novel that our story is based.

About the Creators

Rey Terciero, also known as Rex Ogle, has written and edited hundreds of books and comics for children and young adults. He is a queer writer who has always been drawn to strong female protagonists, including Elizabeth Bennet, Princess Leia, Jean Grey, and Hermione Granger. *Meg, Jo, Beth, and Amy* is his debut graphic novel.

Bre Indigo is a lover of astronomy, salmon sashimi, and open minds. She tells stories of gentle boys, tough girls, and those in between, with a focus on tolerance and the many faces of love. You can find her ongoing webcomic series *Jamie* online at Tapas.

Gabrielle Rose Camacho is an aspiring artist and devoted cat lover. As this is her first big published project, she hopes to see more to come in paving the way for her career.

Johana Avalos Merino, better known as JAMpoots, is a Chicanx artist based in SoCal working on comics that deal with identity and the journey it takes to find one's self.

Joanne Kwan is a graphic artist and webcomic creator with a penchant for the odd and obscure. She has a passion and respect for history but is far from traditional and enjoys straying off the beaten path. All of her series can also be found online at Tapas.

Ryan "Toxin" Thompson is the creator of the fantasy webcomic series *Fauna Fairest* and *Drop Devil*. He has a profound love for all things colorful and a passion for exploring stories of growth and self-discovery. He tries to live a quiet life, far out of reach of the dangerous magical creatures he so often tells tales about.

A Larger World Studios is Dave Lanphear, Troy Peteri, and Joshua Cozine. They're letterjacks for comic book publishers all over the world. Join them online at Twitter and Instagram @A_Larger_World!